521

P9-CCU-867

Books by Matt Christopher

Sports Stories

THE LUCKY BASEBALL BAT
BASEBALL PALS
BASKETBALL SPARKPLUG
TWO STRIKES ON JOHNNY
LITTLE LEFTY
TOUCHDOWN FOR TOMMY
LONG STRETCH AT FIRST BASE
BREAK FOR THE BASKET
TALL MAN IN THE PIVOT
CHALLENGE AT SECOND BASE
CRACKERJACK HALFBACK
BASEBALL FLYHAWK
SINK IT, RUSTY
CATCHER WITH A GLASS ARM
WINGMAN ON ICE
TOO HOT TO HANDLE
THE COUNTERFEIT TACKLE
THE RELUCTANT PITCHER
LONG SHOT FOR PAUL
MIRACLE AT THE PLATE

THE TEAM THAT COULDN'T LOSE
THE YEAR MOM WON THE PENNANT
THE BASKET COUNTS
HARD DRIVE TO SHORT
CATCH THAT PASS!
SHORTSTOP FROM TOKYO
LUCKY SEVEN
JOHNNY LONG LEGS
LOOK WHO'S PLAYING FIRST BASE
TOUGH TO TACKLE
THE KID WHO ONLY HIT HOMERS
FACE-OFF
MYSTERY COACH
ICE MAGIC
NO ARM IN LEFT FIELD
JINX GLOVE
FRONT COURT HEX

Animal Stories

DESPERATE SEARCH
STRANDED

Stranded

Stranded

STRANDED

by
Matt Christopher

Illustrated by
Gail Owens

Little, Brown and Company
Boston   Toronto

FIRST EDITION

T 10/74

Library of Congress Cataloging in Publication Data

Christopher, Matthew F
  Stranded.

  [1. Survival--Fiction. 2. Shipwrecks--Fiction.
3. Blind--Fiction] I. Owens, Gail, illus. II. Title.
PZ7.C458St   [Fic]   74-6365
ISBN 0-316-13935-1

Published simultaneously in Canada
by Little, Brown & Company (Canada) Limited

PRINTED IN THE UNITED STATES OF AMERICA

To Ruth and Charles "Bus" Reniff,
and Mochica

Stranded

1

The thirty-one-foot sloop, *Excalibur,* was heading in a south-southeasterly direction from Great Exuma Island in the Bahamas, having already spent three weeks among the numerous cays that stretched out for ninety-two miles from New Providence Island to the southeastern tip of Great Exuma.

Up till now there had been no indication of impending foul weather. A wind had been blowing from the north-northeast at a steady fifteen knots per hour, providing ample power for the craft's leisurely journey: first to Great Inagua, then around the Caicos Bank, the easternmost tip of the route, finally to return to the outer islands on the way home.

A check with the coast guard before leaving

George Town at the southern tip of Great Exuma had assured her three-member crew, Andrew and Mary Ann Crossett, and their twelve-year-old son, Andy, of good sailing weather for the next few days, providing nothing unpredictable happened. So far only an accidental grounding in the shallow waters of the Jumento Cays had delayed them about half a day. To free the sloop Andrew Crossett had carried the plow anchor some one hundred feet astern in a power-driven dinghy, dropped it into about five feet of water, then returned to the sloop and tried to winch it back into deeper water. It was a tough, grinding operation, even with Mary Ann and Andy's help. When at last the sloop broke loose, the Crossetts continued on their journey, this time with extra caution.

They anchored on the leeward side of Castle Island for the night, then set off at daybreak for Great Inagua.

It was just past ten that morning when the radio announced a storm warning.

"A tropical storm has developed about a hundred miles east of Mayaguana Island and is heading in a westerly direction at about fifteen to twenty knots an hour," the announcer said.

4

"A *tropical* storm?" Andy whispered. The thought suddenly sounded scary.

"Wait, Andy," said his father. "Let's hear the rest of it."

"The diameter of the storm is predicted to be at least fifty miles and probably as wide as a hundred. The damage that it could cause to anything in its path is nothing short of disastrous. The coast guard warns that all vessels within the area head for safer waters as soon as possible."

"I don't like the sound of that, Andrew," said Andy's mother worriedly.

"Neither do I, Mary Ann. Get me the chart. I'll change course right away."

Traveling with the Crossett family on the sloop was Max, Andy's pet dog. Max had been with Andy constantly since the Crossetts had found him, almost four years ago. Though he had never been trained as a Seeing Eye dog, he acted as Andy's second sight. For Andy was blind.

It wasn't entirely for Andy's sake that his parents had embarked on this extensive journey through the Bahamas. Andrew, Andy's tall, blond, robust father, had lived by the sea and sailed boats ever since he was in his teens. A long cruise some-where — though he had never planned exactly where — had been a dream of his for years. Then he read about the Bahamas, about the trade winds that kept the climate moderate, and about the hundreds of sandy beaches and sandbars off which excellent snorkeling could be enjoyed. Though sightless, Andy could enjoy the sailing too. It was no problem for him to man the tiller as long as there was someone nearby to direct him which way to turn it. And he was an excellent swimmer. His parents knew he would enjoy swimming in the buoyant salt water of the ocean, and he loved to fish.

But there was another side of Andy, a side that had often worried Andrew and Mary Ann Crossett. For a long time after Andy had become blind — a firecracker had destroyed his eyesight when he was nine — he had withdrawn into a shell, refusing to see his friends. "I wish I'd die," he had said to his father one day. "I might as well be dead. I can't do anything anymore."

"You're wrong, Andy," his father had tried to reassure him. "There is still a lot you can do. You have all of your other senses: smell, taste, feeling,

6

and hearing. You also have us — your mother and father. And you have Max. We'll be your eyes."

The waves had grown high and perilous by four o'clock that afternoon. Dark, cumulonimbus clouds were advancing from the northeast at a rate of almost twenty knots an hour. The sloop rode the crests like a fragile box, then sank into the troughs, lifting again on the next crest as water raged furiously up over the deck and cockpit.

In a short time the sky above the small craft was black. The loud, howling wind billowed both the mainsail and the Genoa jib, battering the boat with hard, angry thrusts as if trying desperately to capsize it. The rain, too, lashed out in savage bursts as if from a giant hose which became intermittently plugged, only to break loose again with another devastating torrent. The halyards whipped against the mast, and the ship's joints quaked in protest.

Andrew Crossett sat in the cockpit, both hands on the tiller and feet braced against the port locker to keep himself secure. The yellow slicker he wore glistened with water, as did his weary, grimacing

face. His orange life jacket was tight around him, and the bottom of his pants and his white sneakers were soaked.

A little while ago he had sent Mary Ann down into the cabin with Andy and Max and asked her to call the coast guard, to notify them of the *Excalibur*'s location. They were somewhere near the northwest coast of Great Inagua Island.

Now his thoughts returned to his decision to sail down here in the first place — the birthplace of the tropical storm, the cyclone and the hurricane. Of course he had not considered the possibility of running into any one of them; there were meteorologists on the job every minute, and radio reports at regular intervals. But even so he hadn't listened to the reports every time they were broadcast, figuring that the possibility of a tropical storm developing was one in fifty.

But now here it was, and he and his family were in the middle of it.

The vertical hatch cover lifted and Mary Ann stepped out, a life jacket over her yellow slicker, its hood tightened around the oval of her face.

Andrew stared at her. "Mary!" he shouted. "Get back into that cabin!"

As if she hadn't heard him, she dropped the cover and sat down on the starboard locker, the rain pelting her slicker.

"Mary! Did you hear me?" Andrew shouted again.

"I heard you," she answered calmly.

"Don't you think you should stay with Andy?"

"Andy's all right. He's lying down, and Max is with him."

"Did you get the coast guard?" Andrew asked, his voice softer.

"I don't know. I didn't get an answer," she said. "I just kept on calling. I don't know whether or not anyone heard me. There was a lot of static."

Mary Ann looked over her shoulder at the clouds, which were advancing so fast that they looked like a black canopy sweeping across the sky. Then she looked beyond the starboard bow of the sloop, and Andrew caught the worried gaze in her eyes.

He remembered the long discussion they had before they had planned the trip. Like he, Mary Ann enjoyed the sea, but she had always preferred to tag along, never really caring to learn very much about the fundamentals of sailing. Andrew had always wished she would take more interest, but he knew that he couldn't force her. He was pleased that she was willing to participate with him as much as she did, knowing that she did it because of the bond between them — their love together and their mutual love for their only son, Andy.

However, when it came to the Bahamas trip, Andrew didn't think these reasons were quite

10

enough; she would have to have some genuine interest in going. But when he suggested they call it off she insisted that they mustn't. "Now now. Don't worry," she had said. "Once we get going, I'll enjoy it, too."

And she had. Up until now, she had enjoyed every minute of it. He could tell by the laughter in her voice and in her eyes. He could tell by the things she said, the tone of her voice and every move she made.

Now Andrew looked away from her to the task at hand. Never before in his life had he been so worried. On the other hand, the boat seemed big and durable enough. She weighed slightly over eight tons, with a two-ton keel and a five-foot two-inch centerboard designed to maintain stability in very rough seas. She had two twenty-five-horsepower diesel engines in case she needed them: sails might tear under severe wind conditions, although it was rare, and on northern trips the winds might calm down to nearly zero, though here in the tropics that was practically unheard of.

"Land, Andrew! Land!" Mary Ann shouted suddenly.

He looked in the direction she was pointing, and when the huge waves lifted the boat to the peak of their crests, he saw a hump on the horizon. It was still very far away. Too far, perhaps.

Max, lying on the forward berth next to Andy, heard Mary Ann's cry and lifted his gray, dark-spotted head. His long white ears perked up and his heart thumped. He listened for the cry to repeat, but when it didn't, he relaxed and looked at the soft, quiet face of the boy beside him. The boat was pitching and yawing so violently that Max had to keep bracing himself so as not to fall against Andy, whose eyes were closed as if in sleep.

Max had been selected by Andrew Crossett from a litter of five English setters. He was a year old when Andy lost his sight, and ever since that day he had been as devoted to Andy as any animal could possibly be to his master. Max was big and lean, with a shiny gray coat that suggested good health. His long ears, the only completely white parts of his body, draped over the sides of his angular face like furry curtains. His eyes, like his ears, were sharp and keen.

Suddenly the boat struck something hard and careened wildly, knocking both Andy and Max

12

against the portside bulwark. Andy's first reaction was to reach for Max and encircle him tightly with his arms.

"Max! We hit something!" he yelled.

There was another stunning blow, which sent boy and dog sprawling on the floor, and then a distant scream which Max's sensitive ears picked up. He immediately sensed that something terrible had happened, and began to utter a shrill, whining cry. He struggled to keep from falling all over his young master, but Andy was holding him tightly in a panic-stricken grip.

One of the dangers threatening ships sailing among the many outer islands of the Caribbean is the reefs that encircle the islands and extend for hundreds of yards, sometimes miles, into the sea. Seamen check their charts carefully and steer clear of them. Andrew Crossett knew about the reefs from his close study of the chart, and under normal circumstances he could have avoided them.

But late this afternoon with a hurricane turning the sea into a boiling cauldron, drenching the sloop with rain, and hurling it mercilessly in its deadly path like a plastic bottle, Andrew Crossett completely lost control. He had seen the reefs and had tried to steer the boat clear of them, but it had been a backbreaking, futile struggle.

The first impact was a severe jolt that would have knocked him off the boat were it not for his tight grip on the tiller. He cursed, and realized he should have insisted that Mary Ann go back into the cabin. But it was too late now.

He grabbed the boom which was swinging back and forth wildly, and released the tiller. The pulleys were straining at their joints, and the mainsail was torn from the severe lashing it had received from the now nearly one hundred-mile-an-hour winds.

"Mary Ann!" he shouted. "Try to get into the cabin!"

She was sprawled on the cockpit floor, thrown there by the collision. Now she braced herself against the sides, put a hand on the tiller and was reaching for Andrew's legs, when the boat struck another reef. At the same time a huge wave smashed against the starboard beam and lifted it, and Mary Ann, trying desperately to hang onto the tiller, lost her grip and was thrown into the sea. Her shrill scream was terror filled as she sank into the white, frothing water.

Andrew froze in horror as he saw her go over. He glimpsed her in her orange life jacket bobbing up in the water, saw her hand reaching up and heard her voice screaming above the din of the storm. Her cries knifed into his very soul, and he knew instantly that he must try to save her. There were reefs beyond her, but if he could get to her — praise God — perhaps there might be a chance for both of them.

In an instant, he let go of the boom and dove into the water.

2

The second jolt sent Andy and Max hurtling to the floor, and caused a wide crack in the portside of the hull where water was now pouring in. When he felt it, Andy yelled in terror, and began to cry as he struggled to his feet, only to be knocked down as the boat lurched again.

Soon the water was three to five inches deep, sloshing all over the floor, the walls, the berths. Only the long heavy keel was keeping the boat from capsizing completely.

From his blind world, Andy reached out and groped for his dog. "Max!" he cried. "Where are you?"

Suddenly he felt a wet mass of hair, then the warmth of Max's tongue as the dog licked his hand. He was instantly relieved feeling Max beside

him. But what had happened to the boat? Had it sprung a leak?

Andy's throat choked with fresh tears. Were Mother and Dad still in the cockpit, he wondered. Were they okay?

He clutched a handful of sheet and mattress while he held his other hand around Max's neck to keep from falling down on the floor again. But it hardly made any difference. The boat was yawing and pitching, heeling far over on its side and lurching right side up again, and then yawing and pitching some more so that he scarcely knew which side was up. Now he was too terrified to cry.

Suddenly the boat lurched again, and Andy lost his grasp on the mattress. He was knocked back against the wall behind him, his head bumping against it so hard he winced in pain. His feet slid out from under him so that he was sitting on the floor. His arm, still around Max, had dragged the dog down on the floor beside him, and he felt the water slosh up over his thighs, shoulders and face.

"Mom!" he shouted, choking back tears. He waited a few moments, and shouted again, "Mom!"

He heard nothing but the water sloshing inside the boat and the boat's joints creaking as if they were breaking apart, and from outside the shrill, eerie scream of the undying wind.

How long was it going to last?

It seemed to Andy that he sat there for hours. He had expected the water to get deeper, but it hadn't. He didn't know what he would have done if it had.

Now he felt another jolt as something else suddenly rammed against the portside of the boat. This time the impact wasn't as severe as before, but the boat tipped a little more, so that the water level was up to his chest.

Andy was still, depending on the only two

senses that could help him now — feeling and hearing. By now the craft was rocking gently back and forth like a cradle, and the terrible wind had died down. The storm, he was sure, was over.

"Mom! Dad!" he shouted in desperation, and listened for an answer.

There was none, and a horrifying fear came over him. Were they safe and just unable to hear him? *Or had they drowned?*

He started to pull himself to his feet. "Outside, Max," he said firmly.

He hung on to the dog's collar as the dog scrambled to his feet. The water was up to Andy's thighs as he let Max lead him through the door and past the galley. A couple of times Andy slipped, once gulping the salty water into his mouth and quickly spitting it out again, then stumbling over pots, cups and dishes that had fallen to the floor.

Max paused, leaning firmly against Andy's left leg, and Andy felt for the ladder that led to the cockpit. He ascended it and soon felt the clean, warm wind brush against his face and ruffle his hair.

"Mom! Dad!" he called anxiously.

He heard the calls of sea gulls flying overhead,

and the sound of water lapping up against the boat, which was almost still now. From nearby came the soft whispering sound of the wind rustling the branches of trees and foliage. Other than that the silence was deadly.

A cold, shuddering spasm then took hold of Andy. He found the side of the cockpit, sat down and buried his head in his arms.

Max watched him. One ear perked up and then the other, and his head tilted. He, too, had looked around for Andy's parents, but had not seen them. This was strange. They had never left the boat before without taking him and Andy. Something was terribly wrong.

After a while Andy lifted his head. He reached out his hand and the dog took a step forward and placed his head under it, then sat on his haunches. Though it trembled a little, Andy's hand felt tender and warm.

"The storm must have washed us up on an island, Max," Andy said.

A soft whine came from the dog's throat, and he looked about him as if he understood what Andy had said. Overhead, branches of dense foliage grew from the precipitous bank where the boat was wrecked. Underfoot was pure white sand.

A humming sound came from some distant place. The dog pricked up his ears, and lifted his head.

"Hear something, Max?" Andy asked. Then, a moment later as the sound grew louder, he added, "Yes! I hear it, too! It sounds like a motorboat, Max! Or maybe a helicopter! Maybe they're searching for us!"

A loud, resonant drone came from above them now, and seemed to be slowly swinging around in an arc. The dog strained his eyes, but could not see anything through the thick foliage. Suddenly Andy scrambled to his feet and began to shout excitedly, flailing his arms as he did so. "Help! We're down here! Please see us! Please!"

The dog watched him curiously, then rose to his feet and began to bark and wag his tail, as if this were expected of him. He didn't know that no one but the boy could hear him, or that no one flying in the rescue helicopter above was able to see the boat because of the thick foliage hiding it.

Seconds later the sound grew quieter and quieter as the helicopter flew back to its home base. Max looked at Andy and saw the look of despair on the boy's face.

"It's gone, Max," Andy murmured wistfully. "Do you suppose they saw us? They might have. Maybe they'll send a boat after us."

He sat down again and reached for Max's head, found it and petted it. Max looked at the boy's blind eyes sadly, and saw the tears that glimmered in them. A whimper came from him, and he lifted his head and licked Andy's face, tasting the saltiness of the tear that had dropped on Andy's soft, hot cheek.

*   *   *

Almost two miles away, around several jutting reefs, east of the small sandy beach upon which the sailboat had been washed, Mary Ann Crossett was anxiously administering mouth-to-mouth resuscitation to her husband. During those moments of unbelievable terror, when she thought that she would surely die, Andrew had swum to her and held onto her while the mad, boiling sea had tossed them back and forth until it had washed them both up on a reef.

But by that time Andrew had been hurt. She remembered that he had groaned as if in pain, then had passed out almost immediately after they had climbed to the safety of the reef. Fear-stricken at first because she thought he had drowned, she had listened to his heart and heard it beating. Believing that he was unconscious from swallowing so much seawater, she had begun quickly to try to save his life.

Now she heard the sound of a motor, and when she turned saw a coast guard rescue boat pull up near the reef. Immediately two men hopped out of it. One held a line to keep the boat close to the reef; the other knelt beside Mary Ann and her husband.

"I'm Captain Melburg, ma'am," he said. "Are you all right?" He was about twenty-five, with a mustache, and he was wearing a blue coverall with the symbol of the rescue team over his left breast pocket.

Mary Ann nodded, fear for Andrew's life caught in her throat. And her son Andy. . . . Had the boat been smashed on one of the many reefs? Had Andy — and Max — been victims of that dreadful storm?

"His leg is broken," Captain Melburg observed. "We'll have to get him to a hospital."

He got up and turned to a third man standing in the cockpit of the motorboat, saying, "Bill, bring out the stretcher."

Mary Ann started to rise to her feet. The reef was slippery, and she almost fell. The captain caught her in time.

"Come on," he said. "I'll help you into the boat."

"Wait," she said hoarsely, clutching his arms. Her hair was wet and straggly; strings of it clung to her face. "My son, Andy and his dog — they were in the boat. Did you find it?"

"No, ma'am, we didn't."

"That helicopter. They didn't see it, either?"

He shrugged. "I'm sorry, ma'am. They saw you and your husband here and reported to us. They said nothing about a boat."

Fear gripped her. "Then they might still be in the boat! They might still be alive!"

"Could be, ma'am. But we didn't see any boat on our way here. And I'm sure that if the guys in the chopper saw it, they would have reported it to us. I — I'm afraid, ma'am, that it —"

She started to sob.

"Come on," the captain said. "Into the boat. We better get your husband to the hospital as quickly as possible."

He helped her off the reef and onto the boat where the third man waited to assist her. She sat

24

down in the cockpit, and silently watched her husband being brought onto the boat on a stretcher.

As she looked at Andrew's quiet, pale face, she suddenly saw in it a picture of Andy grown up.

Andy, my son! I should have stayed in the cabin with you!

But if she had, she reflected despairingly, she might have drowned with him. *If* he had drowned. Or — unless the boat had been entirely demolished — they *all* might still be alive and well.

She grabbed Andrew's hand and clutched it tightly. It was cold and very limp.

3

The sun was edging toward the rim of the horizon; like a round red palette it furnished pigment for the brilliant crimson clouds around it. The wind had shifted slightly, and was coming now from the northeast. The branches of the trees were rustling overhead, and sea gulls were flying about, now and then swooping down to the water for sighted fish.

Max rose from near Andy's feet, looked at the blood red sun, then stepped up on the roof of the boat and walked to the prow. He looked about him, at the trees, the jagged reef, and the white sand.

"Max," Andy said. "Max, come here."

He turned and walked back to Andy and put his face on Andy's lap. "Getting restless, Max?"

Andy asked, petting him. "Want to get off the boat for a while? Come on. Let's go."

Max barked agreeably, and led Andy to the starboard side of the boat. He stopped there expertly, his tongue hanging thin and long from his mouth, while he waited for Andy to feel his way over the side. The boat was lying on its side because of its long keel, so climbing off was easy.

Max watched Andy step carefully onto the sand, his feet sinking several inches into it.

"Okay, Max," said Andy. "Your turn next."

Gingerly, Max hopped off the boat. The sand was cool and damp, and he lifted first one paw and then the other, shaking each before putting it down again.

"Let's go farther up on shore, Max," Andy suggested. "Let's find out what's in front of us."

Max led him to the jagged wall of the reef, then stopped. Andy reached out and felt the reef, then walked slowly alongside it, all the time touching the hard, jagged crust. His head brushed against a tree branch and he raised an arm and touched it and the other low-hanging branches.

"I'm sure now we weren't seen by the guys in that helicopter, Max," he said thoughtfully. "Our boat's been washed up against a reef that's hidden under some trees. Isn't that something, Max? Of all the places to be washed up, it happens to be *this* place?"

Max barked, as if he understood and agreed.

He walked alongside Andy now, until they came to a cave. Andy began to walk deeper and deeper into it, feeling the rock walls every step of the way, while Max paused. The cave ended a few feet ahead. There was nothing else in it to explore.

He watched Andy touch the rock ceiling, then the wall that formed a crescent behind him.

"Bet I know where we are, Max," Andy said, a touch of pride in his voice. "We're in a cave, right?"

Again Max barked, then he sat down on his hindquarters and looked back at the boat, his eyelids drooping tiredly, his pink tongue hanging. There was something terribly strange about this part of the journey, he sensed, and terribly wrong.

"Know what, Max?" Andy said. "This seems to be a good place to lie down and rest a while. Let's do that, huh? Then we'll get something to eat from the boat. Okay?"

"Ruff!" Max answered.

Andy lay down on a patch of creamy white rock

and Max crawled up alongside him, snuggling his nose into Andy's armpit. Andy giggled, and pulled Max's head gently onto his chest.

"That tickles, Max," he said.

Max's eyelids quivered as he looked protectively at the boy. He wagged his fur-fringed tail a moment, and then was still. Andy's eyes had closed and he was breathing steadily. Max's eyes closed too, and a short while later both dog and boy were fast asleep.

Max awakened first, startled by a feeling of wetness over his warm body. He lifted his head from Andy's stomach and was instantly struck by a small wave that lapped at his legs like a teasing tongue. Quickly he rose, unable to believe what he saw, for when he and Andy had lain down to sleep the sea had been at least five or six feet away. Now it had risen up high enough to reach their bodies.

It was late at night and the moon was full. Silken clouds drifted across its bright yellow face; a shimmering path of light stretched for miles across the water, and from the small island came the hum of a thousand insects in concert with the rustling leaves.

Andy stirred and raised his head. Although they were in shadow Max was able to see the surprise on the boy's face clearly.

"Max!" Andy cried, scrambling to his feet. "It's the tide! We've got to get out of here!"

The dog's claws scratched the rock as he climbed hastily to his feet. Then, as Andy took hold of his collar, Max headed for the outside of the cave, stepping into deeper water. It was up to Max's neck and Andy's thighs, and the dog proceeded with caution, for the reef was slippery.

Suddenly Andy lost his balance and fell. Unable to hold himself erect in Andy's grip, Max fell too, and for an instant he was completely underwater. Quickly, though, he scrambled to his feet and waited for Andy to find his footing. Then he whipped the water off his head and tried again to walk over the slimy reef.

A loud squeak sounded from the cave behind them. Startled by the sound of leathery wings overhead, Max looked up and saw the creature, a large bat. He paused, watching it curiously.

"I think that was a bat, Max," Andy said, shuddering. "Sounded like one."

Another bat flew by, winging over the ocean

and then back. Max watched it briefly; then, his
curiosity satisfied, continued on.

They climbed up several layers of rock until
they found dry land, and here Max paused and
shook his water-matted fur.

"You've got it made, Max," Andy said amusedly. "All you have to do is shake yourself. I'm a little cold, but I'd better take off these clothes and let the wind dry them out. I know it's night because I can't feel the sun."

Max sat back and watched Andy remove his clothes. After Andy had squeezed the water out of them he stood there, his body pale yellow in the moonlight, and said, "Okay, Max, take me to a small tree. I want to hang these up to dry."

Max looked about him, saw a tree with low-hanging branches nearby, and stepped over to Andy's side. Andy held Max's collar in one hand and his wet clothes in the other and let the dog lead him to the tree. He groped for a branch, found one that was strong enough, and carefully hung the clothes over it. Then he walked around in a small circle, paused, and wiggled his feet into the sand. Max watched him, his ears flopping, as he cocked his head to one side and regarded the boy with curiosity.

"The sand's warm here, Max," Andy observed. "And maybe, being under a tree, it'll be cool during the daytime. Shall we stay here for the night?"

Max whined softly as he watched Andy sit down on the sand. Grass grew sparsely here. Besides the young logwood tree on which Andy had hung his clothes, other trees flourished on the island — madeira, sabicu, cedar and palm. A short distance beyond the boy and the dog, a hill rose like a giant camel's hump to a peak of about a hundred feet. The island was no more than two miles long, and like other Caribbean islands was inhabited by wild goats and green turtles, as well as birds, lizards, chameleons, iguanas, bats and raccoons.

Andy began to dig a long, low trench in the sand. When he was finished, he stretched out full length in it, pushing some of the sand away from his feet to give himself more room. Then he pulled some of the sand back over his body and chuckled at his ingenuity.

"There, Max," he said proudly. "I've got me a bed. Go to sleep now. We'll eat when the sun wakes us up."

Max crawled over the warm sand to Andy, and gazed at the boy's face. He looked relaxed. But suddenly tears glimmered at the corners of Andy's eyes, and an arm came out from under the sand and sought the comfort of the dog. Max crept closer, bending his head down low so that Andy could put his arm around him. As he listened to the boy cry, a sympathetic whimper came from his own throat. He didn't fall asleep himself until he saw that Andy was finally quiet and breathing heavily.

They awakened the next morning with the sun blazing over the hill and the never dying wind rustling the leaves. Andy climbed slowly out of the trench, the sand rolling off his body.

"Wonder if my clothes are dry, Max," Andy said, and started to walk in a direction away from the tree. Quickly the dog trotted to his side, and Andy reached down and took hold of his collar.

"Good boy, Max," Andy said as the dog led him to the tree where the clothes were hanging.

Andy felt them and exclaimed happily, "They're dry. I'll wash the sand off and put them on."

He turned so that the sun was at his back, then headed directly for the beach. Max got up and trotted after the boy, who, without his help, had found his way to the water.

"Ah! Soft sand!" Andy cried elatedly. "I did it, Max! I got to the water on my own!"

He waded into the water up to his thighs, washed off the sand that clung to his body, then swam a while. "Speak, Max!" he yelled. The dog responded and Andy turned toward the sound and came out.

He headed toward the tree on which his clothes were hanging, but was missing it by several feet. Max ran to him, brushed up against his side and Andy reached for his collar.

"Thanks, Max," he said. "Okay. To my clothes."

Max led him to the tree, and waited while Andy removed his clothes from the branch and put them on. "Now's the tough part, Max," he said. "Let's go to the boat. I'm starving. How about you?"

Max barked, and led Andy to the water, turning to the left where he remembered they had come from last night. The sandy beach ended where a jagged section of reef began, and Max led Andy onto it, crossing the reef slowly and carefully.

At last they arrived at the boat. Max led Andy into the layer of water on the boat's deck carefully, although it was only about six inches deep. Once aboard Andy found the opening into the cabin without difficulty, and climbed down into it. Max followed him, his tail wagging furiously, for he was hungry and knew that he would soon be fed.

As Andy waded into the water on the cabin floor, he bumped into two boxes of cereal, lying open, their contents spilled and floating on the water. Jars of jelly and jam were also strewn about, but their lids were still sealed. A loaf of bread, unopened, and another, half opened — the slices soggy and shredded — floated near the jars.

Andy lifted out the jelly and jam and the un-opened loaf of bread and carried them out to the cockpit. Then he returned to the galley and lifted the lid of the left-hand seat. It was filled almost to the brim with canned goods, sugar, salt, bread, dog food and a variety of other food staples. He lifted out several cans and a can opener and carried them topside, then returned for a plastic container of drinking water. His last load was some cups and dishes, and a knife and spoon.

After resting for a while he carried the supplies off the boat, taking as many items at a time as he could, and placing them beyond the reach of the water. When he was finished, he poured a cup of water for Max, which the dog lapped up thirstily. Then he filled his own cup. Waiting for something to eat, Max patiently watched Andy tear open a box and pour a part of its contents into a bowl. It was his favorite brand of dog food, and he tore into it with gusto.

Andy laughed. "Easy, Max," he cautioned. "You'll choke gulping that down so fast."

But Max paid no heed, and in a few moments the bowl was empty, cleaned of its last crumb.

Then Max sat back and licked his chops while he watched Andy open up a can and smell its contents.

"Peas!" Andy said. "Ugh!"

He poured a small portion of it into a dish, then opened up another can and smelled it. "Ravioli!" he cried gleefully. "That's better!"

He poured half of the can into the dish, judging the amount by placing his right forefinger into the can. Then he relaxed and ate. When he was finished he picked up his dish and Max's bowl and washed them in the sea. Suddenly his face brightened up as if he had just thought of a brilliant idea. He took off his shirt and piled as much of the food and utensils in it as he could, then tied them into a bundle and slung the bundle over his shoulder.

"Okay, Max," he said. "Back to our tree."

They returned to the tree, Andy walking more surely now than he had on his two previous trips. He emptied the bundle beneath the tree and returned to the shore for the rest of the food.

"This will take care of us a couple of days," he said to Max, but the last word almost died on his lips. Max detected a sad note in his master's voice, and saw the changed expression come over his face. The dog stood quietly by as Andy sat down with his back against the tree. Then he lay on the sand, out of reach of the sun, and looked at Andy with sad, mournful eyes.

"They must have drowned, Max," Andy said, after a moment. "Both of them. They must have fallen off the boat and drowned."

Max rose from the sand just enough to creep forward a few steps.

"You know, I think Mom and Dad knew that I was getting to the point where I didn't care about anything anymore," Andy went on. "But being blind really isn't the end of the world, Max. Like Dad said to me one time — I still have all my other senses. He and Mom and you were my eyes. Well, you're the only one who can be my eyes now, Max."

He reached out his right hand, and Max licked it, then put his head against it. He whined happily as Andy stroked his head and his ears, and he crawled on Andy's lap and began licking his cheeks until he had the boy laughing hysterically.

At last Andy got up, took his shirt off the tree, and put it on.

"Come on, Max," he said. "Let's walk along the beach. First, though, I need a pole."

Max barked and wagged his tail, the tip of it thumping against Andy's legs as the boy turned and started to walk farther inland, his hands stretched out before him like a sleepwalker. Max trotted up beside him, once leaning against the boy's legs when he was in danger of walking into a tree.

Andy raised one hand high over his head and kept the other stretched out in front of him. His raised hand touched a branch of the tree, bypassed it and felt for another. He wrapped his fingers around this one, and gave a soft cry of triumph.

"This one will do, Max!" he exclaimed.

Max stared at Andy, then at the limb, wondering what his master was up to. Ears pricked up and head cocked, he watched Andy break off the limb and strip it clean of its tiny branches. The limb, about four feet long, was almost as straight as an arrow.

"Okay, Max," Andy said, satisfied. "I've got my pole. Let's head for the beach."

Max barked, and ran ahead of Andy until he reached the water. Then he turned around and watched Andy follow, poking the pole against the ground in front of him for any obstruction that might be in his way.

They walked along the shore in the opposite direction from where the boat rested, and abruptly the sandy beach stopped as a steep grade began. Max now strode alongside of Andy, keeping between him and the rising cliff. Scrub brush and wild berry bushes dotted the terrain. A lizard skittered from a bare rock and stopped behind a bush, peering with bulging eyes and raised head at them.

Max stared at it, then broke loose from Andy, barking furiously as he lunged after the tiny reptile. At the same time Andy, startled almost out of his wits, lost his balance and started to fall. The lava-like rock on which he stood crumbled, then gave way beneath him, and he went over the edge. A panic-stricken scream tore from him as he sailed out into space, one hand still holding onto the pole, the other grasping vainly at the air.

4

When Max heard Andy's cry, he stopped in his tracks and whirled around. Motionless, he stared at the spot where he had left his master just seconds ago. His body trembling, he gave a yelp and bounded toward the edge of the cliff.

On the very edge of it he paused and looked down. In the brackish-looking water below he saw Andy's flailing arms and again heard him yell. Without another second's delay Max leaped.

His tail and ears flared up as the wind rushed by him, his four feet stretched out stiffly. He dropped with a loud splash a couple of feet from Andy, swallowing a little water as he sank below the surface. Stroking hard, he rose back up, shook his head vigorously, then swam straight for the boy. Andy, although an able swimmer, was obviously too shocked to know in which direction the shore was. He cried out in relief as Max reached him, and ran his hand along Max's back to his tail which he grasped tightly.

"Okay, Max!" Andy cried. "Head for shore!"

Max obeyed, Andy trailing like a human caboose. They soon reached the shallow water where Andy let go of Max's tail and scrambled to his feet.

"Go fetch the pole, Max," he commanded. "It's in the water back there."

Max, standing up to his belly in the water, looked where the boy was pointing, then took a bounding leap and swam out again. He looked for the pole, and had nearly given up when he saw it bouncing on a wave less than ten feet away. He swam eagerly after it, and clutching it between his teeth he swam with it back to Andy. On the beach he dropped it at Andy's feet, then began shaking himself vigorously.

"*Good* dog," Andy said as he picked it up. "*Real* good dog. But you were *bad* when you ran away from me on top of that hill. You startled me, Max, and we were so close to the edge. The next time we're climbing a hill let's keep farther away from the edge. Okay?"

Max whined, knowing he was being reprimanded, and licked Andy's face in order to get back into his master's good graces. Andy chuckled and stroked the wet head, and the dog snuggled up against him, his tail thumping the warm sand.

"What did you see up there?" Andy asked. "Was it a snake? A bird?"

Then Andy touched some of the scratches on his left leg, and put his fingertips to his tongue.

"Scraped my leg going over the cliff, Max," he said. "I guess it's not bad, though. There's hardly any blood."

With modest curiosity, Max smelled the wounds and began to lick them.

Andy smiled as he pushed Max away. "No, Max!" he said. "I don't need your tongue to heal my leg. It isn't that bad."

Max drew back, unhappy, when suddenly something flying by caught his attention. It was a yellow butterfly, and he went after it, chasing it up toward the brush and trees where, at last, it eluded him for good. Disappointed, he turned back, looking for more fun, then ran down to the beach and plunged into the water, the cool wetness feeling good against his warm body. He swam out about twenty feet, then swam back in. Thirsty, he started to gulp down some of the salty water but spat it out quickly.

"Come on, Max!" Andy shouted to him. "Let's take a walk! Maybe there's a house someplace on this island!"

Max shook himself, then ran eagerly to Andy who had gotten to his feet and was waiting with his pole. Again, with his free hand on the dog's collar, Andy let Max lead him over the strange, sandy, brush-covered terrain.

"Just remember where our home base is, Max," Andy reminded him. "That's where our food is, you know."

Soon they reached a clearing where the grass was thick and a cluster of sabicu trees flourished. Max paused and looked out over the sea, and for a moment an expression of sadness came into his eyes. His ears pricked up slightly as if he were hoping to hear voices he hadn't heard in quite some time, then he felt a tug on his collar and went on.

"Bark if you see a house, Max," Andy commanded.

Max peered hard into the distance, first to the left, and then to the right, but there was no house within sight, nothing but shrubbery and trees, and a few flying sea gulls in the vast, blue sky. The heat was bearable because of the constant wind that swept in from the sea. But the sun itself was hot, and its rays were taking their toll on Andy's face, arms and legs.

After having walked for a couple of hours, Andy had Max lead him to the part of the shoreline nearest them. Andy removed his clothes and waded into the water, Max splashing in beside him. When the water was up to Andy's chest he sprang forward, ducking his head and swimming out, with Max close behind. A school of fish darted out of their way. On the sandy bottom a pair of angelfish hovered about a large brain coral. Lurking near another coral were a couple of Spanish hogfish and a lone crab that burrowed into the sand.

Suddenly Andy gave a startled cry. "Max!"

The dog looked at him and saw that Andy had stopped swimming and was treading water. His face was paper white.

Max swam up closer, looking quickly in the water around him to see what could have frightened the boy.

"A fish brushed by me, Max!" Andy cried softly. "A *big* fish! Probably a shark! Or a barracuda!"

It was a barracuda, about five feet long. From

farther out it had seen the white flesh of the boy approaching from the shallow depths near the shore and had swum toward him, curious. When it turned away briefly so as not to be struck by Andy's slowly stroking arms, it had brushed up against the boy's body.

"Swim slowly, Max," Andy advised quietly. "Just swim slowly."

Below and slightly behind them, the barracuda watched with growing curiosity. Its long lower jaw dropped gently, exposing rows of sharp teeth, and then closed. Swinging around toward the boy and the dog, it swam after them, maintaining a distance of about five feet behind them. Finally it paused as it saw the boy touch the bottom with his feet and walk away, with the dog right behind him.

The barracuda remained there until it saw a fish that looked like an appetizing morsel near a brain coral, and forgetting the boy and the dog, swam after it. The little fish darted underneath the coral and into a crevice just in time to save itself from the deadly jaws. Disappointed, the barracuda whipped his tail around again and swam toward the deeper part of the sea in search of bigger and, perhaps, easier game.

"Lucky these scratches weren't bleeding, Max," Andy said, his heart beating fast as he collapsed onto the sand. "Whatever that was — a shark or a barracuda — it might have tried to make a meal of my leg."

He shuddered and put his head in his hands. Max shook himself, then sat back and watched. A muscle twitched on his chest, and a bead of water dripped off the side of his jaw.

At last Andy lifted his face from his hands, wiped the few tears that had come to his eyes and smiled. Like a happy child, Max snuggled up to him and licked his cheeks.

"I've got to stop crying like a baby, Max," Andy said, rising to his feet. "I've got to remember I'm twelve years old and big enough to take care of myself — with your help, that is," he added, smiling. "Come on, let's head back for the tree. I'm starving. How about you?"

Max barked and romped ahead of Andy in the direction of the tree. They had wandered almost a mile away from it, and the sun was long past its zenith when they were finally within sight of it once again.

Suddenly the dog stopped. Something — a weird looking beast — seemed to be foraging in the boxes. It was an iguana, one of the island's rarer reptiles. This one was about four-and-a-half-feet long.

"Max! What is it?" Andy yelled. But Max was running after the reptile, barking furiously at the creature that had invaded their territory and was stealing their food.

The iguana lifted its short, blunt head at the sound of the barking, and fixed its bulging eyes on the dog charging across the patches of grass toward it. For a moment the scaly skin under its neck bulged like a pouch, then receded. Its large mouth opened, and its long tail snapped. The

iguana began to back away, dragging its tail, its eyes still fixed on Max.

In an instant Max was upon the lizard, lunging past its opened mouth to get at the area behind its head. The dog sank his teeth into the tough, scaly hide, but lost his grip as the iguana rolled over on its side, all four legs pushing against the dog. Then Max went after the reptile's belly, sinking his teeth into its leathery skin, and again the iguana rolled over, all four legs lashing desperately to push the dog off.

Suddenly it broke loose and bolted into the brush, its tail swishing back and forth. Max ran after it, barking viciously. He reached the brush and found himself blocked by a wall of thick, leafy vines. He tried to crawl underneath as the iguana had done, and succeeded in getting his head through. But thorns dug painfully into his hide as he tried to pull the rest of his body through. Discouraged, he backed out and ran along the bush, looking for an opening, but found a tangle of thorns too thick to penetrate.

Finally he quieted down; his ears still strained for the sound of the iguana, but he heard nothing except the wind and the surf behind him.

He brushed his mouth across the sand to wipe

off the blood from his bout with the lizard, spat out the sand that had filtered in, then turned and trotted back to the tree. As he sniffed at the boxes and canned food, his acute nostrils picked up the iguana's scent once again, and a growl rumbled from his throat.

He heard a soft sound and looked up to see Andy advancing slowly toward him, poking his way forward with the pole.

"Max!" Andy called softly. "Max! Are you all right?"

Max whined to assure the boy that he was, then ran up to him and nuzzled him happily, his body wiggling and his tail wagging. Andy crouched, laid down the pole, and put his arms around the dog's neck. Hearing Andy's words of endearment and affection, Max licked at the boy's face and damp hair and tried eagerly to crawl up onto his lap, whining like a happy puppy.

5

It was after they had slept a while underneath the tree, Max's back against Andy's, that a sound brought the dog awake. It was a soft, high-pitched sound — *ha! ha! ha! ha! ha! ha!* — like that of a tiny animal or bird in distress.

Max raised his head, his eyes and ears instantly alert, and listened.

When the sound came again, without even a glance at Andy, Max bounded off silently toward its source. He had gone only about ten yards when he saw the creature — a young sea gull. Its dark gray head lay on the sand, and one of its bluish gray wings was spread out like a fan beside its body.

Max paused about ten feet away and stared at

the bird, cocking his head first to one side and then to the other. When he sensed that the sea gull was injured, he approached it gingerly.

The gull's eyes, which had been shut, suddenly opened. Startled, the bird raised its head, let out a screech and made a frantic, desperate attempt to fly. But it managed to move ahead only a couple of feet.

As Max watched, the bird jerked its head one way and then the other, as first one eye and then the other appraised him.

"Max!" Andy called. "Max! Where are you?"

Max glanced over his shoulder, then back at the gull, caught between two demands at once.

"Max!" Andy called again. "Can you hear me?"

Max glanced over his shoulder again and barked. Then he advanced slowly toward the sea gull, his long ears hanging nearly over his eyes. Suddenly the sea gull made an attempt to leap away, but Max sprang forward, jaws opened, and caught the gull by its back. Getting a firm, but gentle, grip on the bird so that his teeth wouldn't hurt it, Max picked it up and carried it to Andy.

"Max," Andy said, reaching out a hand. "What have you got there?"

Max dropped the sea gull on the grass in front of Andy. A cry from the nervous, frightened bird told Andy where it was; he touched it, running his hand gently over the small, feathered body, and then picked it up.

"I bet it's a laughing gull, Max!" he said excitedly. "Mom and Dad read about them to me! Oh — oh. It's got a broken wing. We've got to fix it, Max. We've got to feed and take care of it until it's able to fly again. Right?"

Max barked, his eyes fixed proudly on the sea gull as if it were his prize.

Andy felt the bones under the injured wing again, then brought the wing gently back against the plump little body.

"When we go back to the boat I'll try to find our first aid kit," he said. "Right now I think we ought to give it something to eat."

Holding the sea gull against him, Andy reached over toward the boxes of food that lay nearby and picked up a box of cereal. He found a bowl, poured a tiny amount of the cereal into it, then added a little water from the can.

He placed the bowl on the ground and held the sea gull near it, talking to it and trying to encourage it to eat. At first the sea gull looked cautiously this way and that, but then it gave in. The gull's red bill snapped up one of the grains of cereal; its head lifted; the gull waited a moment, then snapped up another grain, and another, while Max whined and thumped his tail happily.

* * *

At the hospital on the island where Andrew and Mary Ann Crossett had been taken, X rays revealed broken bones in both of Andrew's legs. They were put in plaster casts and Andrew was ordered to remain under hospital care for at least three or four days. He had lacerations and contusions that received medical attention, too. Mary Ann had been treated for shock, exposure and lacerations. The one thing that the attending physicians couldn't do was heal their wounded hearts.

But neither Andrew nor Mary Ann had accepted the belief that their son and Max had drowned in the storm. Since their boat had not been found, they still staunchly believed that Andy and Max were alive.

The tropical storm had reached hurricane force, an official of the volunteer Air Rescue Association explained, and every one of their planes was in use checking for lost boats and people. Every vessel of the United States Coast Guard was out on the seas involved in the same task. "As soon as your sailboat is spotted — if it hasn't wrecked and gone down — it will be checked immediately," the Crossetts were told. "That's all we can do. In the meantime, all you can do is pray."

Andrew and Mary Ann had been put into separate rooms, but on the second day Mary Ann was well enough to sit in a wheelchair, and she visited Andrew in his room.

"How are you feeling, Andrew?" she asked, taking his hand in hers and squeezing it gently.

"Lousy," he said.

"It's my fault," she said, feeling a lump in her throat. "If I had stayed in the cabin with Andy and Max this wouldn't have happened. I wouldn't have fallen overboard, and you wouldn't have gone after me."

"Mary Ann, please," Andrew pleaded. "You can't think it's your fault. And you're with me. At least we're both safe."

She looked at him, her pale face framed by her black hair. "Do you think they've drowned, Andrew?"

"No. I *know* that boat. It was built of strong fiberglass and could take a lot of beating. I know."

"But, if it were filled with water, could it have sunk?"

"I'm not sure about that. It could have. But," he added hastily, pointing a finger at her to emphasize his point, "we weren't too far away from shore, Mary Ann. The way we were being blown that boat would have been pushed up on those reefs before it could fill up with water and sink. It's possible, Mary."

She looked at him miserably, her eyes glistening with tears.

"Thanks, darling," she said softly. "I — I was giving up hope."

He smiled at her. "Don't ever give up, sweetheart," he said. "We'll have our boy and dog back. Wait and see."

*　　*　　*

After having fed the sea gull, Andy considered going to the sailboat and bringing back the first aid kit if he could find it. He would also bring back more food.

But he was worried. Did he dare leave the sea gull? Would it be able to run off with one bad wing? And what about predators? Taking the bird with him was out of the question; he would have his hands full bringing back the first aid kit and the food.

"I know what I'll do!" he cried suddenly, and proceeded to dig out a hole in the sand.

Max watched him curiously, then eagerly began to help. There was something about digging a hole that reminded him of buried bones.

But, when they finished digging, there was no bone. Max looked at his master disappointedly, until he saw the boy place some leaves into the hole and then put the sea gull gently on top of them.

"There," said Andy, pleased at his ingenuity. "A nice nest for you. And don't try to get out. Hear?"

He rose to his feet, brushed the sand off his pants and turned toward the sea. "Come on, Max," he ordered. "Let's go to the boat."

Andy had no trouble finding the first aid kit. It was in the cabinet in the head, where it had been placed when the family had prepared for their long journey.

Suddenly Andy and Max heard a sound. At first it was a hum, then it grew louder as if a swarm of bees were advancing from a long distance away.

"It's a plane, Max!" Andy shouted. "Hurry! Get off the boat! *Let them see you! Let them see you!*"

The dog stumbled and splashed through the water inside the cabin, then bounded out into the cockpit. In his hurry he skidded on the smooth, tilted deck and jumped off onto the rocky shore. By now the plane was directly overhead, shielded from view by the overhanging trees.

"Run out where they can see you, Max!" Andy shouted. "Run!"

The dog ran past the cave and up the shoreline.

He peered up through the trees, and seeing the plane flying off in the distance, he bounded along the beach in pursuit, barking loudly.

But the single-engine plane, its high wing a bright blue, and the words AIR RESCUE written on its fuselage, flew on, oblivious of the boat, the barking dog, and the desperate blind boy on the ground beneath it.

6

It was early the next morning, about six o'clock, when Max's sensitive ears caught the sound of a breaking twig. Andy was still asleep beside him. The sea gull, in its sand hole, had its eyes wide open, but was making no effort to move. Obviously the gull was quite contented among its adopted friends.

His head raised and his ears alert, Max scanned the area around him, listening for more sounds. Suddenly, about fifty feet away, he saw a tan animal about four feet tall, with legs as thin and long as sticks. It was standing beside a bush, a shaft of sunlight playing on its head. Almost at once its eyes met Max's. The animal's short, pointed ears pricked up, then it turned and ran off, its tail bobbing behind him. Out of curiosity, Max took after him.

The animal was a goat, one of the few wild ones inhabiting the remote island. Though it wasn't swift, its cloven hooves allowed it to run over rocks and climb steep hills with agility.

Through tangled brush, briar, and over hard crusts of sharp rock the goat led the dog. When Max reached the top of a tall mountain, the tallest point on the island, he became aware of a new and glorious sight. It was the ocean on the south side of the island. It, too, had a sandy beach, but here the water seemed to stretch to a much greater distance than on the other side. Far away, barely visible to the eye, were fragments of tiny islands, and winking in the sun was the sail of a craft several miles away.

Max looked down at the rough terrain in front of him, his eyes seeking the light brown goat. The animal had stopped and was looking in his direction, as if waiting to see what he was going to do. When Max saw it, he took off with a leap over a small bush, then on down the mountain. Once he lost his footing on the loose gravel and slid on his back for some ten yards.

When he regained his footing he scrambled

down to the bottom of the mountain. About ten minutes later he came to a halt on a small hill and looked around him. There was no sign of the goat. Discouraged, Max decided to return to his master.

He looked up at the mountain, and, feeling tired now, he decided to walk around it. He was hot from the pursuit — hot, hungry and thirsty; as he walked he snatched a couple of berries off the bushes he passed.

Wandering on, Max looked forlornly at the unfamiliar terrain around him. Was he heading in the right direction? The foliage around him was as thick as a jungle. Briars had scratched his face and thistles had lodged in his fur. He was also limping from a pain in his right front paw, where he had not known it, but on his way down the mountain he had cut it on the sharp edge of a stone during the chase.

Finally he came to a cliff overlooking a sandy beach and a small lagoon. He looked down at the beach; it seemed far below him. But the sand was soft, and Max jumped. To his surprise, he suddenly discovered himself up to his shoulders in the sand. Although the cool dampness was a welcome relief at first, Max realized he was still sinking.

He yelped and lifted his head high, his eyes

glazed with fear. Peering around him, he whined imploringly, and struggled to free himself from the quagmire, all four legs churning frantically. A sea gull flew overhead, then swooped down to get a closer look at him. Max looked up at it, then looked away miserably, knowing that such a small winged thing could never help him.

Meanwhile, Andy was growing tired of waiting. But he was also a little worried. Max had been gone for nearly an hour. It was the longest that he and Max had been separated since they had been on the island.

He climbed to his feet and headed in the direction that he remembered Max had taken. No doubt the silly dog had seen an animal and had chased after it. But how far had it taken him, whatever it was?

Suddenly sweat glistened on Andy's face as the terrible thought occurred to him that perhaps this time Max had gone after an animal stronger than he. What if Max had caught up with it, fought it, and then — for the first time in his life — lost?

Quickly Andy brushed away the frightening thought, trying to assure himself that Max was a smart dog and would not attack an animal much stronger than he was, unless absolutely necessary.

He kept the pole ahead of him to make sure his path was clear, and held his left arm out to protect his face from any low-hanging branch or tall bush. He walked on for a hundred feet, circling around prickly vines and pausing frequently to call for Max. Sharp needles of scrub brush scraped his legs and tore his pants and shirt, and he began to wonder whether in his dark world he could hope to find his beloved dog.

Each time he yelled for Max, Andy stopped and waited for that familiar, answering bark, but it didn't come. He walked on, stumbling occasionally, and falling once to one knee when he tripped on the side of a large stone.

He rose and hobbled on, listening to the cries of the sea gulls and other island birds. From off to his left came the distant thunder of ocean surf, and he knew that was a sure way of judging his direction. Although he might not be able to retrace his steps to the tree he called his home on the island, at least he wouldn't be too far from it.

He began to climb a hill, realizing that the earth beneath his feet was now ribboned with rock. Suddenly, where he expected to touch hard ground, his pole stabbed the empty air, and a cry tore from him as he lost his balance and began to slip over a sharp ledge. He let go of the pole and groped frantically for something to hang on to.

Luck was with him. His hands found and grabbed a small tree that was growing out of the side of the gorge into which he had almost stepped. With his legs dangling against layers of sharp, projecting rock, he hung there, not knowing that a chasm of some twenty feet in depth yawned dangerously below him.

7

Fear still gripped Max as he struggled to get out of the quagmire. He was inching forward, only his head and part of his shoulders visible above the wet, soft sand. His tongue was hanging from his mouth and he was gasping.

Struggling through the quagmire as if he were swimming in slow motion, his feet at last touched a harder bottom. With the new traction he was able to pull himself out, and soon was on dry land again. He shook himself, shedding blobs of the muddy sand from his coat. Then he glanced around him, gave his head another vigorous shake, and ran toward the sea.

Just short of the water he turned left and continued to run along the sandy shoreline. But the beach was short; he had to cross over onto a reef which slowed him down. Finally he jumped onto bare ground where he was able to run faster. Already his coat was drying in the hot sun, and as he ran through bushes the branches scraped off much of the dried sand.

He was emerging from a shallow ditch when something in his path brought him to a sudden stop. It was an iguana, about half the size of the one he had fought.

An instant later the reptile turned its head and saw him. Then it turned and slithered away under a bush, leaving a trail behind it in the soft earth.

Max watched it make its departure with impassive interest, then continued on his way. At last he arrived in surroundings he recognized, and, barking loudly, rushed to the tree where he had left his master. But when he arrived there Andy was gone.

Max stood looking at the spot where Andy had rested, then walked over to the sea gull which cocked its head and looked up at him inquisitively. The bird's feathers fluttered for a second, and its breast swelled. Then it cried softly and settled down, relaxed to see that the intruder was Max.

Max looked beyond the bird, then walked

around the tree, sniffing at the sand. He smelled the faint scent of the boy and began to follow it, but among the bushes and trees he lost it again. Whining in desperation, he ran this way and that, sniffing hard at the ground, his tail wagging furiously. Again and again he tracked down the boy's scent, and again and again he lost it, each time growing more alarmed. Finally, between barks he heard a cry, and he recognized the voice.

Barking furiously he leaped ahead toward the source of the sound, and soon found himself near a precipitous cliff overlooking the sea. He paused, his eyes scanning the earth around him and then the vast sea.

When the cry sounded again, he looked up, and saw a tree growing from the side of the cliff. He went to it and looked down; there he saw Andy, hands and feet wrapped around a branch of the tree.

Max barked, and Andy raised his head, his face brightening instantly.

"Max!" Andy cried. "Oh, Max! Thank God!"

The dog barked again, whipping his tail furiously and trembling as he stepped close to the brink of the cliff. The sea was almost straight down below him, with jagged reefs edging the shoreline. Max whined, longing to help the boy but afraid of the dangerous drop.

"I'm hanging over a ledge, aren't I, Max?" Andy said.

He started to pull himself closer to the cliff, one hand grasping the tree trunk, the other groping for the edge of the cliff. The dog leaned toward him; his nose touched one of Andy's fingers, and the boy breathed a sigh of relief.

"Good boy, Max," said Andy. "Good boy."

He grabbed the dog's collar, then slowly, cautiously, he let go of the tree trunk and crawled up onto the cliff, with Max doing his best to help. Once on his feet, Andy gently touched the bruises on his knees and shins that he had sustained in the fall.

"I was lucky, Max," he said. "Real lucky."

Max looked up at him, his eyebrows quivering; then he lifted his paws onto Andy's shoulders and lapped his face. The boy laughed and pressed his face against Max's muzzle, crying, "Hey! Where have you been? You're covered with sand!" He grabbed the dog's legs and put him down.

"Come on," he said. "Let's head back to our tree. We'll both take a swim, then eat."

He took a few steps forward, then paused. "Hold it, Max," he said. "I lost my stick. I'll have to get another one. Take me to a small tree."

Max wagged his tail, looked around him, then headed toward a young tree a few feet away. He stopped in front of it, looking up at the boy with pleasure, and barked happily at Andy, who found his way over to the spot. Grabbing the thin trunk, Andy ran his hands down its length. Satisfied, he broke it off near its base, trimmed off the tiny branches and grabbed Max by the collar.

"Now back to our tree, Max," the boy commanded.

As if both Andy and Max had thought of it at the same time, when they returned they approached the sea gull, still nestled in its sand hole. Andy picked it up and held it tenderly against him, stroking its soft, dark gray head and neck. Then he returned it to its nest, and left it some food, while he and Max went swimming. The water washed the sand off Max and refreshed both him and Andy. Afterward they returned to the tree, and Andy fed Max, then helped himself from a can of vegetable soup.

By now very tired, both boy and dog fell asleep side by side in the shade of the tree.

In the middle of the afternoon Max was aroused by a new sound. He lifted his head from his forepaws and pricked up his ears. Soon he detected a scent, and he looked around him, suddenly trembling. In an instant he rose quickly to his feet, a growl beginning in his throat and growing steadily stronger. Just then Andy awoke.

"What's the matter, Max?" he asked. "You see something?"

Max did see something — another dog — a big, black Labrador retriever. The animal was some seventy feet away on the beach, his head held high and his tail stiff. He stood like a statue as he watched Max, and Max watched him, not a muscle stirring in his body.

"Is it a person you see, Max?" Andy asked hopefully. Even as he spoke he rose to his feet and yelled, "Hellooo, there! Who is it?"

There was no answer. The retriever looked at the boy curiously. Then he started to come forward, and the growl in Max's throat grew louder. A muscle along his right shoulder quivered, and his lips curled back in an angry snarl. He lowered his head until it was nearly at a level with his shoulders and back, and started forward to intercept the stranger.

The retriever paused, his neck arched, his jaws tight.

The rumble in Max's throat exploded into a loud bark when he saw that the other dog wasn't going to budge. Instantly Max broke into an angry run, ready for battle. His duty was to protect his master from intruders, and if the retriever refused to retreat by threat he would be forced to retreat by battle.

Max was within ten feet of the retriever when suddenly the big, black animal turned and bounded away. Max slid to a halt in the sand, thinking that he had finally succeeded in scaring off the retriever. But twenty feet down the beach the other dog stopped and looked back. Max watched him, his hackles starting to rise again.

The retriever barked and started toward him, and again Max went after him. Now the stranger turned tail and ran down the beach, back the way he had come. This time, Max, anxious to prove that he meant business, didn't stop the chase. When the retriever arrived at the reef he leaped up onto higher ground and raced on through the bushes. He was fast, but Max finally caught up with him at the bottom of the cliff where not many hours before Andy had had a close call.

He charged at the retriever, going for his throat, but the other dog, the red of battle now flaming in his eyes, lunged back with bared jaws. He clamped his mouth over Max's muzzle and bit down on it, and the setter yelped in pain and rolled over to break himself loose. Again the retriever attacked, seizing Max's thigh in his jaws. Yelping, Max scrambled to his feet and lunged at the retriever's neck, sinking his teeth into it. He lost his hold as the retriever spun away, a streak of crimson on the black fur of his throat.

Suddenly, Max saw a blur of motion out of the corner of his eye, and turned. Two young men were scrambling down the side of the cliff. Both wore trunks over their suntanned bodies and their feet were bare. One was tall and swarthy, the other a little shorter and more muscular.

"He's fighting with another dog, Jim!" the tall one shouted. "Stop it, Rocko! *Stop it!*"

"Let 'em fight, Norm!" Jim yelled. "They're evenly matched. Let's make a bet!"

"Bet? You nuts or somethin'? Rocko will *kill* that dog!"

"So what if he does? He's probably just a stray, anyway."

Jim grinned avidly as he watched the dogs fight.

Norm looked on, worried and disapproving. The animals clawed, bit, snarled; first one would topple the other, then the situation would be reversed. They did, indeed, seem to be evenly matched. After several minutes of fighting, both seemed to be tiring.

Norm advanced toward them. "Come on, Jim. Let's stop 'em. You grab Rocko, I'll grab the setter."

"Man, Norm, I don't know about you," Jim said, his hands on his hips. "You enjoy *my* fights, I hope?"

"How can you compare your fights in the ring with this one?" Norm replied angrily. "Come on, before they kill each other."

He started to reach for Max's collar. Shrugging his shoulders, Jim went after the retriever. Yelling at the animals, the two men pulled them apart.

Max tried to shake himself loose from the grip on his collar, but finally realized it was no use. His heart was pounding, and saliva dripped from his mouth.

Still holding his collar, Norm stroked Max's back and patted him gently on the shoulders.

"Dog, you're beautiful," Norm said admiringly. "Where did you come from, anyway?"

"Anything on his collar?" Jim asked.

Norm looked at the tag around Max's neck. "Yeah," he said, and read, " 'I'm Max. I live at two oh nine Sheffield, Crest Park, New Jersey.' "

"Man! He's a long way from home."

"Wonder where his owner is?"

Max dropped back on his hindquarters to lick at the wound on his thigh. The fur there was thick and matted with blood.

"I hate to let him go like that," Norm said seriously. "Rocko's left him some souvenirs that ought to be taken care of right away, but our first aid kit's on the boat."

"What're you feeling sorry for him for?" Jim retaliated. "Look at the cuts he's given Rocko."

Norm looked at the crimson patches on the Labrador's body which the dog was already licking.

"Looks like they both need first aid," he said. "Jim, what do you say we take them both to the boat, treat them, then sail down along the island?"

"And look for the setter's owner?"

"Yeah."

Suddenly Jim sucked in his breath and his eyes widened. "Norm! The steaks!"

"Oh, great!" cried Norm. "They're probably burnt to a crisp!"

Jim bolted off, running up alongside the steep, slanting cliff. As he ran, he shouted a command to Rocko, who followed immediately. Norm let go of Max's collar and, speaking in the soft, gentle tones of one who understood and loved animals, urged the setter to follow him. Max looked at him, apparently unsure of what to do; then he rose slowly and followed him, limping on his right rear leg from the wound in his thigh.

Finally, they arrived at a sprawling tree under which two huge slabs of barbecued steak, burnt almost black, were lying on a grill. Both dogs gazed at the meat with hungry eyes, though neither made a move toward it. But Jim suggested they give the meat to the dogs, since there was lots more on board for them.

They removed the steaks and put them on the grass, cautioning the dogs to be careful. The animals approached the meat, sniffed it, and then went about devouring the steaks until nothing was left but clean bones.

8

H alf an hour had gone by and Andy was terribly worried. This was the second time that Max had chased after an animal and had not returned right away. But what kind of an animal had it been this time? An ache throbbed in his throat as he blamed his blindness for depriving him of so much. He rubbed violently at his eyes to give vent to his anger, and then began to cry at the frightening thought that Max might never come back.

To be alone on an island, an island where apparently no one except a few wild animals lived, was a terrifying thought, and Andy fell to the hot sand, trembling.

He lay there for several minutes, and suddenly heard a soft, high-pitched sound near him. The sea gull.

Wiping away his tears he reached for the bird and picked it up. Pressing it gently to him and kissing it on the beak, he realized his predicament was like the gull's: he was blind and the gull couldn't fly. A thing that was so important in life for each of them had been taken away. Only a slim hope remained that Andy's sight would eventually be restored — about as much hope as that the gull would fly again.

He knew, too, that he couldn't give up. There was that chance — that one-in-a-million chance — that his mother and father were alive. Someday, he prayed, they would all be together again, and on the strength of that prayer he had to stay alive.

He fed the sea gull some food and water, and applied a small dab of ointment to the wounded wing. Then he gave the gull another gentle squeeze and put it back in its nest.

When he thought of Max again, he stood up and yelled, "Max! Max! Come here, boy! Come here, Max!"

But the cry brought back no sound of Max's familiar, pounding feet and his happy bark. There was only the sound of the wind blowing through the trees, the sea washing the sands on the beach, and the soft beating of the surf against the reefs.

The heat was getting to him, and he went down to the beach. He lay in the shallow water for a long time, until he felt cool and refreshed. When he returned to the tree he went past it purposely, and cried out in pain as he scratched himself on a berry bush. But the shaded ground underneath the bush was covered with a cool blanket of dried leaves, so there he lay down and waited for Max's return.

* * *

By now a thunderhead that had formed in the eastern sky was approaching fast, and the wind had picked up. Norm Addison and Jim Laverne were sticking close to shore on their twenty-one-foot, single-masted sailboat with a dinghy trailing by a rope at its stern. They had considered sailing around the island in search of Max's owner, but the threat posed by the thunderhead made them postpone their trip till it passed overhead.

The rain came, pelting the boat with large drops while the young sailors and the dogs remained safe inside the cabin. Soon, however, the storm passed and the sun shone brightly again, pouring down heat that would have been unbearable were it not for the constant, easterly trade wind.

The young men hoisted anchor, raised sail and began their trip around the island. They traveled in an easterly direction, but, because of the wind, they had to tack to starboard which took them farther away from the island. They sailed straight on for about half a mile, then tacked again, bring-

81

ing the boat to port so that it headed back toward the island. This tack led them as close to the island as they dared to come, and now and then they had to alter their course briefly to avoid hitting the coral heads that penetrated the surface of the water.

Norm manned the tiller while Jim stood on the bow, watching the shore through a powerful pair of binoculars. At Norm's feet lay the retriever, Rocko, holding his head up so that his eyes were just above the level of the coaming. Max had been left in the cabin.

Suddenly, Jim spotted something on shore. "Norm!" he shouted. "A boat!"

"Anchored?"

"No! It's on shore, tipped on its side!"

"A sailboat?"

"Yes! But the mainmast is gone! Looks like it's broken off!"

"You don't see anybody around it?"

"Not a soul!"

"Then that's probably where the setter came from! Let's haul down the sails and take a look!"

Norm steered the boat so that it faced directly into the wind, and Jim dropped anchor. Here the sea was only about two fathoms deep. The sails flapped freely as Norm brought them down and Jim furled the jib. Closing the hatch to the cabin to keep Max safely inside, the two young men got into the dinghy and rowed to the battered boat on shore.

Inside the cabin Max looked up at the closed hatch and whined despairingly. Suddenly his ears pricked up at a new sound coming from outside, and he jumped up on the table and looked out of the narrow window. When he saw the dinghy pass by with the two young men in it, he whined louder and scratched at the window. The sound caught the young men's attention, but Norm smiled and shook his head as he continued to row.

With a pang in his heart, Max dropped to the floor and began to pace it with restless, nervous energy.

The young sailors beached the dinghy and went over to examine the sailboat. They found a badly battered craft with a broken mast, torn sail, and foodstuffs strewn inside the cabin where several inches of water covered the tilted bottom.

"Stinks like a sewer," Jim remarked.

"Sad, sad," Norm said. "They got caught in that hurricane but good."

"That's something," Jim said. "Everybody got thrown overboard except the dog."

"You're drawing a hasty conclusion," said Norm. "Maybe the dog doesn't belong to this boat."

"Okay. But I'm willing to bet he does."

Norm lifted a seat cover and looked at the canned and boxed foodstuffs inside. "Dig this," he said. "Enough to feed an army for a week. And it looks as if you're right. There was a dog on board. Look." He lifted out a couple of boxes of dog food.

"What did I tell you?" said Jim with an I-told-you-so smile. He looked at the contents in the bin and a selfish grin came over his face. "Wouldn't do to let it stay here and rot, would it?" he said, kneeling to lift out some of the food, but something on Norm's face made him hesitate.

"What is it now?" he asked. "Afraid those people might come back to haunt you?"

"I'm just thinking," Norm said.

"About what?"

Norm looked at his friend and shook his head regretfully. "Sometimes, Jim, I wonder if you've got a brain in that muscle-bound skull of yours. I was just thinking about these people dying in those waters. Doesn't that shake you up just a little?"

"Sure it does. I'm human, I have feelings. Now, come on. Let's get these things out of here and into our boat before somebody else gets here, too."

Reluctantly, Norm began to help, and they emptied first one food closet, then the other. It took four trips in the dinghy to carry all the food-stuffs to their boat. The only supplies they left behind were the spoiled meat and raw foods lying in the water.

Max watched with sad, mournful eyes, as the two men stowed the food supplies in their own boat. He started to run toward the ladder, but Jim quickly grabbed him by the collar.

"No, you don't, big pooch," he said, smiling. "You're going to stay with us. You're *our* dog now. And you don't have to worry. We've got all the dog food you'll need for as long as we're going to be here."

He opened up a box, poured a small portion of it into a bowl and placed it on the floor. "Go to it, boy," he said.

Max looked at the food, sniffed at it, then looked up at Jim with heavy-lidded, bloodshot eyes. An ache was gnawing at his stomach — but not from hunger — as he turned away and walked toward the rear of the boat. He circled a small area twice, then lay down, placing his head on his forepaws and curling up his tail so that it almost touched his face.

The young sailor shrugged. "Okay, be stubborn," he said. "Maybe you'll want it later."

He put the box down and climbed out to the deck where Norm was already unfurling the mainsail. In five minutes they were on their way back to the other side of the island.

Some two hundred yards away, under the shade of the berry bush, Andy Crossett was lying fast asleep.

9

Max lay still a long time, hardly changing his position. He felt the movement of the boat, and now and then his eyes lifted to the bowl that had been left for him. But he felt no real desire to eat.

He fell asleep, and whined and twitched, and at last woke up with a start. He looked about him, remembered where he was, and brought himself slowly to his feet. He went to the bowl, smelled the food, and took a morsel of it into his mouth.

Then he looked up at the closed hatch, and listened to the voices of the two sailors and the raucous cries of sea gulls. A frantic urge to get out of this trapped place began to haunt him, and he ran up the ladder as far as he could and barked.

The hatch opened, and he bolted up through it, but a strong arm quickly encircled his neck.

"Just where do you think you're going, dog?" Jim said gruffly.

Max tried to break loose from the hold, but couldn't. Jim chuckled. "Come on. I think I'd better tie you down there."

"Why down there?" asked Norm, who was manning the tiller. "Why not leave him up here?"

"If we're going to Buck Town he might get the notion to run off. You want him to do that?"

"I mean tie him up here. We'll never get to be friends with him if we keep him imprisoned in the cabin all the time."

Just then Max noticed Rocko in the middle of the cockpit floor. The Labrador had risen to his haunches the moment Max had emerged, and was staring at him.

"What about Rocko?" Jim asked.

"He'll sit on the roof of the cabin," Norm replied. "Okay, Rocko. You heard me. Get on the roof."

The Labrador rose and leaped up onto the roof, where he found a satisfactory spot and sat down. Norm grabbed a nylon rope he had loosened from the end of the boom, and tossed it to Jim, who tied one end of the rope to Max's collar and the other to a cleat. It was just long enough to permit the dog to lie down comfortably on the cockpit floor.

The boat sailed on; it was on open water now where there was no threat of coral heads. Buck Town, the sailors' destination, was a small town nestled on a bay on Brent Cay some five miles from the island where the Crossetts' boat had been wrecked. Its one main street was of macadam and badly in need of repair. Side streets were dirt roads lined with small, cement-block houses, vegetable gardens, coconut palms and poinciana trees. Two restaurant-motels overlooked a scenic harbor. It was from one of them that the two men had rented their sailboat, and now they were returning there to replenish their ice supply.

They anchored in the harbor and went ashore in the dinghy, taking Rocko with them. Max was left behind once again, with the bowl of food on the floor beside him, though he still wouldn't eat.

Norm and Jim returned an hour later carrying a tubful of ice between them. They put the ice into the refrigerator, then returned the tub to shore. Rocko got back on the roof of the cabin; the sails were hoisted, anchor raised, and soon the boat was heading out of the harbor and back into deeper waters, a steady ten-knot-an-hour wind billowing its sails.

It was seven o'clock. By nine-thirty it would be dark.

"We sleeping on board tonight?" Norm asked.

"Why not?" Jim replied. "We're loaded with chow. We've seen a lot of good spots to anchor at. Got any preference?"

"Yeah," said Norm. "Wildcat Island. In that cove next to the cliff. We'll be protected there in case a strong wind comes up."

Jim laughed. "Don't you like to be rocked to sleep?"

"Rocked to sleep, yes. But not shaken out of bed."

Altocumulus clouds from the northeast headed in their direction, and soon heavy drops of rain began pelting the boat, its crew and the dogs.

But within ten minutes the sky had cleared and the rain had stopped, just as the young sailors arrived at the cove near the high cliff on Wildcat Island. They dropped sails and anchored about fifty yards from shore, where the water, clear as crystal, revealed a sandy bottom, dozens of brain coral and patches of grass.

Jim and Norm got into their swimming trunks

and went snorkeling, despite warnings from officials at the motel not to swim after six o'clock because of dangerous barracuda. They didn't venture far from the boat, however, and kept within ten feet of each other.

Max raised his head and looked about him. He had seen the two men jump overboard, wearing masks, snorkeling tubes and flippers, but that was several minutes ago and they hadn't returned yet. He looked around for the Labrador, but his position made it impossible for him to see the other dog lying quietly on the cabin roof. A minute later Max began to bite at the rope which held him prisoner on the boat. It felt supple, but even after a lot of chewing it failed to tear apart. Discouraged, he rose and moved to the cleat, looked it over thoroughly and began to gnaw at the coils. Max tugged and yanked, growling angrily when the stubborn rope refused to come loose. But he kept at it, and at last succeeded in pulling it off. In a moment he was free.

He looked around him, panting, his heart beating hard. A low growl behind him made him turn quickly, and he saw the Labrador beyond the edge of the cabin roof, his brown, piercing eyes fixed on him.

Without hesitating, Max leaped overboard, plunging deep beneath the surface of the water and then coming back up, all four feet paddling furiously. He shook the water from his head, looked for the land and swam boldly toward it.

Suddenly he heard shouts from the young men, but he continued on for what would be the longest distance he had ever swum in his life. From his collar the rope trailed like a long, wiggling snake.

Jim, watching the setter cutting a swath through the water, cried grimly, "I can't believe it! Look at him go!"

"Let him," Norm replied. "There must be something — or somebody — back there he wants more than us."

*   *   *

"Mom!"

Andy woke up from his dream, trembling. He rubbed his eyes and sat up. A branch scraped his head, reminding him that he was under the berry bush instead of the tree he had adopted as his home.

He shuddered as he remembered the dream. How scary it had been! He had been sailing with his parents and Max in the *Excalibur* during a severe storm. He had been in the cabin, lying on a bunk, when a strange figure started coming down the ladder. But the figure was blurred, and had no face. It was then when Andy had cried out and awakened.

"Max," he whispered. "Are you here?"

He listened and held out his hand, but Max didn't respond.

"Max!" he yelled, fright gripping him. "Max!"

He crawled out from underneath the bushes, searched for a walking stick and, after several minutes, found one. Then he stood up, still trembling, and walked into the wind, knowing that direction would lead him to the sea.

He knew he was close to the water when his bare feet began sinking into the cool, softer sand. Laying the stick down, he went into the water to refresh himself. He walked out till it was up to his thighs, swam around a bit, then returned to shore. By the way the sun was hitting him, he knew it was getting late in the day.

Andy sat on the beach where the water was shin deep and raised his face to the sky. He held his eyes open, letting the sun shine on them and mirror itself in them like tiny gold coins. "God," he prayed, "please bring my mother and father back to me. And my dog, Max. I love them so much, and I love You."

Hope. There was always hope. He must never forget that.

10

When he felt hunger gnawing at his stomach, Andy walked to the left along the shoreline till he arrived at the reef. Knowing now where he was, he turned and headed up the sand to the tree. Even before he reached it, the soft cry of the sea gull greeted him.

He smiled, set the pole up against the tree and picked up the big bird. He stroked its back gently and talked to it, then felt its injured wing.

"There's only you and me now, bird," he said. "Anyway, till Max gets back. Gee, I hope nothing's happened to him."

The sea gull kept crying, and Andy put it back in its nest, all the time fighting off his anxiety about Max. He got the bird some food and water, then started to make a meal for himself. He opened a can, dipped out a spoonful and tasted it. Ravioli! He dipped into it ravenously, then slowed down as he realized that he had all the time in the world. When he finished he put the empty can into the box where he had put the others, and then rested beneath the tree, dreaming and talking to the sea gull about his Mom and Dad and his happy times at home with them and Max.

All the while he hoped that he would hear an airplane, or the sound of a boat that would mean help was on the way, but he heard no such sound. Nor did he hear Max's familiar bark.

He got to thinking of the food. What would he do when it was gone? How long could he live without eating?

He sprang to his feet and tried to banish the terrible thoughts from his mind. The move startled the sea gull so much that it cried out in fright, fluttering its good wing. Gently, Andy stooped and picked it up, apologizing as he stroked its ruffled feathers. Soon the sea gull relaxed.

Andy put it back into its nest, picked up an empty cardboard box and the pole and headed toward the reef. He might as well get some more cans of food now, he thought. Even without Max to guide him, he knew his way pretty well now.

Though he stumbled on a sharp reef on his way to the boat, and bruised his right leg, it wasn't serious. He climbed aboard the tilted deck and made his way down into the cabin. Stepping into water, he groped for the food locker. As he reached his hand down into it, lower and lower, feeling all around, sudden fright engulfed him.

The box was empty!

Panicked, he dropped the lid with a loud, heavy clatter. Sweat pouring from his face, he groped his way to the other closet, opened the lid, and felt inside it, fingers trembling. As he feared, this too was empty. He dropped the lid and sat down on it, his heart thumping so loudly he could hear it.

Who had been here? Who had removed all the food? And why hadn't he heard them, whoever they were?

Then he realized that the thieves could have come on a sailboat. And they probably had come while he was asleep. Obviously they hadn't cared about who owned the boat, or they would have conducted a search on the island. Then again they might have concluded that the people who owned the boat had all perished in the hurricane.

"But now I'll starve!" Andy cried aloud, his voice like an explosion in the silent cabin. "I'll die!"

He choked back a sob, and wondered if the drinking water had been taken, too. He stumbled to the closet, opened the lid and felt inside it. Relief flowed over him in a wave as he felt two full plastic containers still in there. He removed each one, then carried them out of the boat, one at a time. If he couldn't have food at least he'd have water.

He picked up his pole and one of the water containers and started back to his tree. The five-gallon container was burdensome, and time and time again he had to set it down and rest. At last he made it to the tree, and after resting for several minutes he dug a hole in the sand, placed the container into it, then covered it with leaves to protect it as much as possible from the boiling sun. Then he returned to the boat and retrieved the second container, burying it as he had done the first.

Finally able to rest, he picked up the sea gull and sat with his back against the tree, his face toward the sound of the softly pounding surf. He could tell that the sun had gone down, for it was cooler now. He held the bird on his lap and tenderly stroked its silky back, talking to it for a while, and once again his thoughts wandered to his mother and father, and Max.

A voice in his head tried to tell him to be realistic, to make himself believe the inevitable. His parents were dead, it told him. They had perished in the sea during that violent storm. He shook his head hard and cried out loud, "No! No! I won't believe it! I won't! They're alive! They're alive!"

And what about Max?

Andy gave the sea gull some water, took a drink himself, then placed the sea gull into its nest.

After a while, Andy lay down, and listened to the wind blowing from the east, the rustling leaves, the sea lapping on the beach and the other peaceful sounds of the night. But all these were background music to the thoughts that continued to rage in his mind, thoughts of his parents and Max.

On another small island not far away, Max reached shore. First he walked up on the beach and shook himself, showering the beach with seawater. Then he looked back in the direction of the boat, the Labrador and the two young men for a final time, and began to run along the shoreline, back toward the area where he knew he would find his young master. He had to slow down and walk cautiously when he arrived at the reefs and cliffs; thick foliage forced him to venture deeper inland. But, as soon as he could, he returned to the sandy beach where he could run freely.

Now and then lizards skittered behind the bushes as he bounded by, and a couple of times he paused at the curious sight of sand crabs that burrowed quickly into the sand when they sensed his presence. Then he would run on, sometimes whining softly at the thought of seeing Andy once again.

Darkness fell slowly, and finally Max had to stop and let his bone-weary body rest. He found a spot near a palm tree where the sand was covered with a carpet of palmetto leaves, and here he slept till the early dawn.

He was thirsty when he awoke, and took a swallow of water from the sea. But though the saltiness of it made him even thirstier, he forced himself to run on, never once forgetting his destination.

On one of his detours inland he came upon the ruins of an old building set on top of a hill. Much of the stone roof and the walls had collapsed.

Max advanced toward the building cautiously,

his footsteps soundless on the hard ground. He came around a wall and stopped dead. There, less than ten feet ahead of him, was a large bird feasting on a rat.

The sudden sight and smell of a live fowl and its kill aroused his appetite. The bird, a hawk, continued to tear at the rat's entrails, lifting its head with each bite and devouring the flesh in a single gulp. Max stood stock-still, watching the bird avidly, knowing that the slightest sound on his part would frighten it away.

Suddenly the hawk's head jerked about like a ball on a swivel, as it sensed the presence of the dog. Realizing that he couldn't delay another instant, Max bounded forward. The hawk let out a terrorized screech and leaped in the air, spreading its broad wings. But Max was too fast for it. He caught the bird in midair, clamping his teeth on the thick joints of its left wing, and brought it to the ground.

The setter held the hawk there for a moment, then shifted his jaws quickly to its neck. Soon he felt the bird's hot, throbbing body shudder and grow limp.

He was still eating it when something moved across his line of vision. He looked up quickly,

blood dripping from his jaws, and stared into the ugly, bulging eyes of an iguana. A growl rippled from Max's throat, but the iguana didn't move. It stood there like a statue, head held up high. Suddenly its neck enlarged like a balloon, and then receded. As Max watched the reptile he remembered his victory over the first iguana he had encountered not long ago. He knew he had nothing to fear from this one either.

After several moments, the iguana turned and wobbled away, its leathery, pointed tail dragging on the earth behind it.

Left again to himself and his prize, Max went about finishing his breakfast.

At last, his hunger satisfied, he relaxed and wiped the feathers off his jaws with his forepaws. Then he got up and worked his way back to the shore where razor-sharp reefs and tangled foliage continued to make the going difficult. He came upon a family of crabs and, curious, began to nuzzle one of them. Instantly a pair of claws snapped at him, making him stumble backward on the slippery reef, but he soon regained his balance and went on.

At last he reached the end of the island, but nothing yet had looked familiar to him. He paused on a jagged reef and looked across a narrow channel of water to a neighboring island. The channel was about a hundred feet wide; the water was dark green, and looked rough and menacing. But his powerful instinct to return to Andy forced him on.

Max leaped into the water and swam hard against the current sweeping in from the open sea. By the time he was halfway across the current had washed him closer into the cove. Now, as he headed for the island, the sun was in front of him, low and blinding. At last, when nearly all his strength was gone, he reached shore. As he climbed up on a reef, he slipped and fell back into the water, sinking beneath its surface. He nearly panicked, but he stroked hard to pull himself back up; finally his head bobbed out of the water and he was able to fill his lungs with fresh air again.

Finally on dry land, he shook the water off his coat, and continued on, remaining close to shore. Soon he reached a cliff and recognized it as the one from which he had helped save his young master. Now that the terrain looked familiar to him he barked happily and ran faster and faster. Before long he would be at the tree where he had left Andy.

11

A coast guard vessel left the marina at the island where Andrew and Mary Ann Crossett were hospitalized, crossed the harbor, and passed through a narrow strait. Its destination was the island where the Crossetts had been discovered a few days ago. The crew was almost certain that the boat, the boy and the dog had perished in the hurricane, but Andrew and Mary Ann had insisted that they conduct a search.

As the rescue boat motored along the leeward side of the island, an officer on board maintained a constant watch with binoculars, finally noting the spot where they had picked up the Crossetts. They cruised on another mile, becoming more positive than ever that the boy and his dog were lost for good.

Moments later the officer cried out: "A boat! In front of that cave!"

The crew captain took the binoculars and looked, too. "You're right!" he exclaimed. "Okay! Let's head in and take a look!"

He steered the vessel toward shore and minutes later anchored it some twenty-five feet from the tilted, battered *Excalibur*.

The two officers and a third crewman motored their dinghy to shore and climbed aboard the wrecked sailboat, examining its damaged hull, broken mast and torn sails. When they entered the cabin, they found the food lockers stripped almost bare.

"Somebody's been here before us," the captain observed.

"The kid, maybe," a crewman remarked.

"It's possible. But the kid is blind, remember. It would take him some doing to empty this boat of all the food the Crossetts said it was carrying."

They left the boat and walked up the side of the hill. On level terrain they paused and the captain cupped his hands around his mouth.

"Helllooooo!" he shouted. "Hellloooo!"

From his place near the berry bush Andy thought he heard a new sound. He listened hard. There it was again! A human voice!

His heart pounding, he scrambled to his feet and shouted back, "Helllllooooo! I'm down heeere!"

"Keep yelling, so we can find you!" the same voice answered.

Andy continued to call to them, and a few moments later he heard feet pounding on the turf.

"Dad!" he cried, tears burning in his throat. "Oh, Dad!"

Soon a pair of hands touched his shoulders. "This isn't your dad, son," a calm voice said to him. "It's Captain Melburg of the United States Coast Guard. You're Andy Crossett. Right?"

Trembling, and immediately saddened that the man wasn't his father, Andy nodded. "Yes. Then you — you never found my father . . . and mother?"

"Oh, yes, we've found them," the captain replied. "They're in the hospital."

"Hospital?"

"Don't worry. They're both okay. Your father broke both legs.

"And my mother?"

"She's fine. She had wanted to come along with us — they both did — but we thought it was better that they stayed behind. Come on. I'll pick you up and carry you. . . ."

"No!" Andy cried, drawing back from the hands that began to encircle him. "I can't go with you now!"

The captain frowned. "Why not?"

"My dog Max is gone! He's somewhere around, but I don't know where! I can't go without him!"

"Have you tried calling him?" the captain asked.

"Yes!"

"How long has he been gone? A few minutes? A half an hour?"

"No."

Andy hesitated. He realized if he told them how long Max had been gone, the captain might conclude that Max was gone for good and refuse to look for him.

"How long?" the captain asked again.

"Not long," Andy answered finally.

There was a pause. Then the captain said, "Bill — Frank, yell for the dog as loud as you can."

The two men called Max's name, waited a moment, then called it again. But Max was nowhere in sight.

"He probably won't come now because he might be afraid of those voices," Andy said.

"Then you yell for him," replied the captain.

Andy tried to, but his exhaustion and the ache in his throat made yelling impossible.

"Come now, Andy," said the captain. "Tell me the truth. When was Max last here?"

"Yesterday," Andy said softly.

"Yesterday? So he's been gone overnight. Do you think he might have chased after an animal?"

"Yes."

"You have any idea what it was?"

"No."

There was quiet for a while.

"Andy," the captain said at last, "we can't stay here, not knowing where your dog is or what has happened to him. Let's be reasonable about it. Don't you think he would have come back to you if he was all right?"

Andy thought about it. "But there's nothing he can't lick!" he cried. "Nothing!"

"He must have tangled with something," the captain said. "But for the life of me I can't figure out what it could have been. There are some iguanas and wild goats on this island, but those are the only large animals. Maybe your dog got into a fight with an iguana."

"He got into a fight with something yesterday — or maybe it was the day before," Andy said.

"But you don't know what it was."

"No."

Silence again. They were probably looking at each other, Andy thought, trying to decide what to do about him.

"Andy," the captain spoke again, "we just can't hang around here all day. You're pretty well sunburned and should see a doctor. Some of our men will search the island thoroughly for your dog, but we can't do it now. Okay?"

Andy thought again. "Okay," he answered reluctantly. "But I'm going to take the sea gull with me. I can't leave it here with its wing not healed up yet."

"Sea gull?" inquired the captain.

"Yes. It's in a nest I made for it."

There was a moment's pause, then the captain said, "Oh, yes, I see it. Okay, Andy. I'll get it for you."

A few seconds later the captain put the sea gull

into Andy's arms; then he picked up boy and gull in his own arms and began carrying them back to the dinghy. On the way he asked Andy to tell about the hurricane. Andy explained it all as much as he was able to, including how he had discovered the foodstuffs gone from the boat.

"Then you hadn't carried it all out yourself?" the captain said.

"No, sir. Somebody else did," replied Andy.

"You know what could have happened, Andy?"

"What, sir?"

"Whoever took the food could have taken your dog, too. They probably tied him up so that he couldn't get away."

Andy's mind turned to other thoughts, too, of what could have happened to Max. "Maybe whoever it was had their own dog," he said, "and when it came around Max went after it. I remember that he barked for a minute, then stopped, then ran off and barked again. Finally I couldn't hear him anymore."

"You could be right, Andy," said the captain gently.

"Do you think I'll ever find him?" Andy asked, feeling a pang in his chest.

"I wouldn't give up. Maybe we can help."

"How?"

"By broadcasting a special bulletin over the radio to all the boats around the islands. If he's on one of them we'll find him, you can bet your boots on that."

Andy smiled. He liked the captain, and from the sound of his voice, he knew that the captain meant every word he said.

But how long would it take them to find Max? Maybe those owners of that other dog were already on their way to other islands. There were hundreds of them in the Caribbean. Or maybe they had ended their trip and were on their way home, never to be seen again.

12

From where he stood on the cliff Max heard the voices calling him. He barked in answer, and began to run as fast as he could along the rough shoreline, slowing down only when reefs forced him to. Then he ran inland, keeping parallel to the sea, and at last arrived in familiar territory. He barked happily, and continued running in leaps and bounds to the tree where he had last seen Andy.

But when he arrived, barking to announce his arrival, Andy was not there. Nor was the sea gull.

Max whimpered pitifully and began to sniff the sand, his long, fur-fringed tail held out tensely behind him. All at once he caught a scent, and his tail began to whip back and forth, excitedly. Barking loudly, he raced across the terrain, past trees and scrub brush and at last arrived at the other end of the beach.

The trail seemed to end there, and a mixture of confusion and disappointment overwhelmed him. He raced about in frustration trying to track down the scent.

Suddenly he heard a sound coming from the cove. He looked up, saw a boat skimming across the water some three or four hundred yards away; then he looked away again. A boat was the least of his interests at the moment.

He ran back up the hill, retracing the scent, his tail wagging furiously. Then he returned to the beach, and was overwhelmed again by frustration.

He paused, listening. There was a change in the sound of the motor boat. He looked toward the sea, panting, his heart beating like a drum. The boat was turning. It was heading back toward the island.

Andy heard Max's barking the minute the sound of the boat's motor quieted down. A shout of joy burst from him, and he almost lost hold of the sea gull which he had been cuddling against his chest. The sea gull cried out nervously, startled by the boy's sudden cry.

"I told you he'd come back!" Andy shouted happily. "I just *knew* he would!"

The captain ordered his crewmen to go in the dinghy to fetch the dog, but then he changed his mind. "Never mind, guys," he said. "The dog's swimming out to us."

Andy could hardly wait. He stood in the cockpit, the sea gull crying softly in his arms. Then he heard that familiar whimper, and felt the boat rock as the men lifted Max out of the water and into the cockpit.

The captain took the sea gull from Andy's arms. "I'll hold him, Andy," he said. "It'll be kind of hard to hold onto two pets at the same time."

Andy's throat tightened as he let the captain take the sea gull from him. Then he opened his arms for Max, who climbed all over him, licking his face and whining like a long lost child who had come back home.

Forty-five minutes later they were at the hospital. Andy, a lump filling his throat, paused in the doorway of a room in which he heard his mother and father talking.

Then he ran in. "Mom! Dad!" he cried, as he fell into first his mother's and then his father's arms. They hugged him fiercely, holding on to him as if they wanted to make certain they wouldn't lose him again.

"Thank God!" Mary Ann Crossett whispered happily.

"What about the sea gull?" Andrew Crossett asked Andy after the boy had told his parents about finding the bird. "Do you want to take it back with us?"

"I've got to," Andy answered seriously. "Its wing hasn't healed up well enough yet to let it go on its own. Anyhow, it and Max have gotten to be pretty good friends."

Max, sitting on the floor near Andy, barked and wagged his tail, as if he approved completely.